W9-CDX-882

Alabaster's Song

For Austin, Caroline, and Claire Green.
May you always hear the song of Bethlehem.

Text copyright © 1996 Max Lucado.
Illustrations copyright © 1996 Michael Garland.

Published in Nashville, Tennessee, by Tommy Nelson®, a Division of Thomas Nelson, Inc.

Library of Congress Cataloging-in-Publication Data

Lucado, Max.
    Alabaster's Song / Max Lucado ; illustrated by Michael Garland.
        p. cm.
    Summary: On Christmas Eve, a six-year-old boy listens to the angel from the top of the family tree sing just as he did on the first Christmas night.
    ISBN 0-8499-1307-1 (original hardcover)
    ISBN 1-4003-0146-7 (4½ x 5½)
    ISBN 1-4003-0007-X (box set)
    [1. Angels—Fiction. 2. Christmas—Fiction.] I. Garland,
Michael, 1952—   ill. II. Title
PZ7.L9684A1 1996
[E]—dc20

96—14749
CIP
AC

Printed in China

02 03 04 05 LEO 5 4 3 2 1

Alabaster's Song

Christmas through the Eyes of an Angel

MAX LUCADO

Illustrated by Michael Garland

Tommy NELSON

www.tommynelson.com

A Division of Thomas Nelson, Inc.
www.ThomasNelson.com

I was six years old when I met the angel called Alabaster. That was a long time ago. I'm grown up now and have a little boy of my own. But I still remember Alabaster.

Here is how I first met him.

My parents put our Christmas tree near my room. I could see it through the doorway. When everyone thought I was asleep, I would lie in bed and stare at the lights and count the shiny balls. I would watch the color glimmer on the icicles. And I know this sounds a little funny, but I would talk to the angel.

High atop the tree he sat. He had feathery white wings and a golden halo. I knew he wasn't real. Well, at least I *thought* he wasn't real. But he looked so friendly with those red chubby cheeks and bright eyes. He looked young. Maybe that's why I talked to him. All my brothers and sisters were older than me. He was the only one in the house my age.

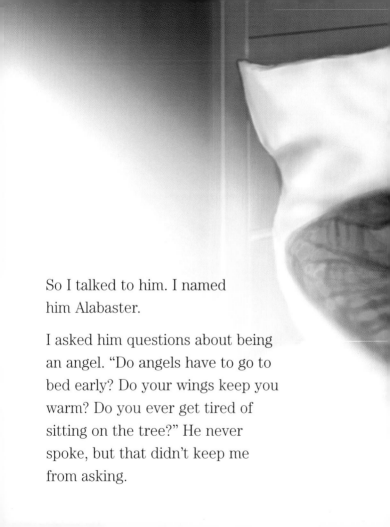

So I talked to him. I named
him Alabaster.

I asked him questions about being
an angel. "Do angels have to go to
bed early? Do your wings keep you
warm? Do you ever get tired of
sitting on the tree?" He never
spoke, but that didn't keep me
from asking.

One night when I was in that in-between
place between being asleep and awake,
I asked just one more question.

"What was it like to see Bethlehem?"

That must have been the right question.
Suddenly Alabaster was standing beside
my bed!

"It wa*th* wonderful."

His face was round, and his eyes were bright. His golden halo and white feathers glowed and sparkled. He talked to me like we were old friends. And when he spoke it sounded like he was missing his two front teeth.

"It wa*th* a great night. We went to the *th*perd*th* becau*th* they were awake. They were *tho* ni*th*e. Mo*th* the time they thought we were *th*ars. But that night, they knew *th*omething *th*pecial wa*th* in the air." He giggled with a giggle that made me giggle, too. By now I was sitting on the edge of my bed.

"What did you do?"

"We ju*th th*ang. Want to hear it?"

"Yeah," I said.

And from that little angel came the most beautiful music. He put back his head and filled our house with a melody only heaven had heard and only heaven could make. He sang and sang like God himself was listening. I put my head on my pillow and listened until I opened my eyes and the sun was up and it was Christmas morning.

"Get up!" It was my dad shaking me. "Come and see your presents."

I jumped out of bed and ran to the tree. There was everything I'd asked for. I was so excited I forgot all about Alabaster and his song.

Soon all the presents were opened, and we all sat around talking and laughing and looking at the new stuff. That's when I heard the song again. Alabaster's song. The room was full of it.

I looked up. Little
Alabaster was on the tree
with his head back and his
mouth open. He was singing.
Just like he had the night before.
I looked around at my family. No one
else was looking at the angel. They were all
talking like nothing was happening.

"Do you hear the singing?" I asked my dad.

"No."

"Do you, Mom?"

"No," she answered.

No one else heard him. But I heard him, as clear as if I were on the tree next to him. His head was turned toward the window, and he was singing to Jesus, just like he had done that first night in Bethlehem.

The next Christmas, when I was seven, I heard him again. And the next. He would stop at my bed on Christmas Eve and sing. And from the top of the tree on Christmas morning, he would sing to Jesus. Every year I saw him. Every year I heard him. Then I got older.

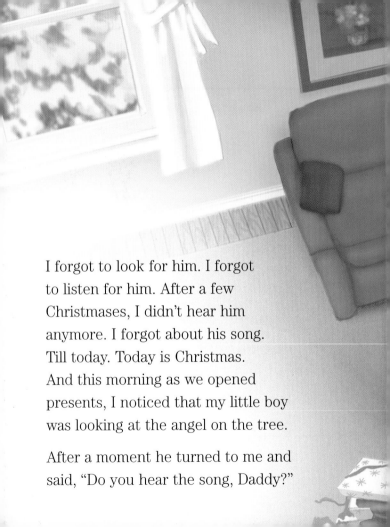

I forgot to look for him. I forgot
to listen for him. After a few
Christmases, I didn't hear him
anymore. I forgot about his song.
Till today. Today is Christmas.
And this morning as we opened
presents, I noticed that my little boy
was looking at the angel on the tree.

After a moment he turned to me and
said, "Do you hear the song, Daddy?"